P9-CEA-816

POOF!

by John O'Brien

Boyds mills Press

For Hannah
—J. O'B.

Text and illustrations copyright ©1999 by John O'Brien

Published by Caroline House
Boyds Mills Press, Inc.
A Highlights Company
815 Church Street
Honesdale, Pennsylvania 18431
Printed in China

Publisher Cataloging-in-Publication Data

O'Brien, John.
    Poof! / written and illustrated by John O'Brien.-1st ed.
    [32]p. : col. ill. ;   cm.
Summary: Two lazy wizards resort to all sorts of tricks in order to get
out of doing simple chores around the house.
ISBN 1-56397-815-6
1. Wizards—Fiction—Juvenile literature. 2. House
cleaning—Fiction—Juvenile literature. [1. Wizards—Fiction.
2. House cleaning —Fiction.]   I. Title.
    [E]—dc21 1999 AC   CIP
Library of Congress Catalog Card Number 99-60226

First edition, 1999
The text of this book is set in 24-point Berkeley Book.

10 9 8 7 6 5 4 3 2

The wizard and his wife sat napping in the parlor.

They sat and napped and sat and napped some more.

When suddenly . . .

"It's your turn to change the baby," said the wizard's wife.

"Yes, my dear," said the wizard with a wave of his wand. "But. . ."

"It's your turn to feed the cat."

"You're certainly right about that, dearest one," said the wizard's wif

"But . . ." She waved her wand over the cat.

"If you recall, you're supposed to walk the dog."

"I would, my little honeybunch," said the wizard as he waved his wand out the window. "But . . ."

"You wouldn't want me to walk the dog in the pouring rain, would you?"

"And why not?" said the wizard's wife. "For isn't it true . . ."

". . . that ducks like to get wet?"

"So right you are, my precious," said the wizard
as he waved his wand upward. "But . . ."

"Without a roof there's plenty of rain for our duck right here, inside."

"But lovey-poo, my clothes are getting soaked,"
said the wizard's wife.

"And so are mine, sweetie pie," said the wizard.

They sat and got wet and they sat and got wetter
until the wizard's wife said . . .

"Let's not sit here in wet clothes.
Let's change into something more comfortable."

So the wizard stood up and waved his wand.

And the wizard's wife stood up and waved her wand. And . . .

The three lived quackily ever after.